A FLIGHT OF BIRDS

A FLIGHT OF BIRDS

by

TIMOTHY HANLEY

Drawings by John Morton Sale

MACDONALD : LONDON

First published in 1953 *by*
Macdonald & Co. (Publishers), Ltd.
16 *Maddox Street, W.*1
Made and printed in Great Britain by
Purnell and Sons, Ltd.
Paulton (Somerset) and London

For
Seumas and Liam
with love

I

The concentration camp was a very large one, but although it was crammed with prisoners there was yet one remaining portion of the grounds away from the huts where it was possible to get a minimum of solitude. This was a small patch of rising ground on which a few gnarled pine trees grew, not far from the tall barbed fence where the German S.S. sentries kept up their endless march to and fro.

It was possible to look beyond this terrible barrier into the distant country—even to ignore it if you fixed your gaze long enough on the greater distance to where, amid the dark wooded country, the faint silver glimmer of a lake could be seen.

To this place most evenings at about sundown a girl dragged herself to sit at the foot of one of the trees, and to gaze, not with hope or even longing, for these emotions had long since gone from her, into this far-off line of country. For this and one other reason she came each night. Sometimes a line of wild swans would fly over towards the lake. The German soldiers would shoot at them, but, having only rifles, they had so far been unable to hit one, and the swans, being wary birds, had not bothered to alter their line of flight but only flew at a greater height, so that now as they passed over they looked like a silvery trail in the sky, and the girl could no longer hear the singing harp-like throb of their wings.

Sitting there with her face turned up to the sky, she looked pitifully pale and thin, her great dark eyes, melancholy as a caged animal's, innocent and infinitely sad. She was dressed in a striped prison gown, ragged and too big for her. The wind blew her lank black hair back from her face, her hands were clasped in her lap. She looked very young—almost a child. Her name was Tamara and she was a gipsy.

Watching for the swans, she said to herself softly as if talking to a child: " Presently they will come. I think they will be sure to come tonight, my six wild swans—the beautiful swans."

As she stared up into the sky another figure approached her, an old man, moving slowly and painfully, dressed as she was, in a striped prison garment. He was very thin and had a ragged black beard. She looked up at him as he kneeled beside her.

" Maman Josef wants you in the hut," he said. " The child is dead."

The girl gazed at him and put her hand up to her brow.

"Ah, the little Baba, the little child," she sighed. " I'll come."

She rose and helped the old man to his feet. As they began to move away she paused and looked up at the sky again.

" Wait—they are coming. The swans. I felt sure they would tonight. There—do you see them? There they are, very high. Look, over the tree-tops."

The old man peered upwards and shook his head.

" I cannot see them," he said; " my eyes cannot see very far now. I can only see the tops of the trees; I can see them moving in the wind, but I cannot see the sky at all."

" I can see them," said Tamara. " They are flying in a line one behind the other: one, two, three, four, five, six—no, there are seven! Oh, Jantsi—there are *seven* swans. Seven! How beautiful they are! They are flying to the lake. Seven swans tonight—another one must have joined them!"

Her face was rapt, but the old man pulled at her arm.

"We must not stay," he said apprehensively; "the guards might see us. Come—we want to bury the child tonight while there is still time. The grave is dug."

The girl turned to him, and they moved away slowly across the bare ground, upon which the roots of the trees could be seen standing out like sinews as if the very ground were starved. They walked a little grotesquely as if propping each other up.

The inside of the hut was crowded with men, women and children, all dressed in the striped prison clothes or in a ragged assortment of ordinary garments. All were thin and dirty, and they sat around or merely wandered aimlessly from place to place; some were lying on the floor of the hut, others lay in built-in bunks that lined the walls.

In one corner was a little huddle of people kneeling and leaning over something on the floor. As Tamara and the old man approached some of the group looked round at them and parted a little to make way for Tamara who went straight to the bowed figure of a woman in the centre. She put an arm round the woman, who did not look up but leant weakly over into the girl's embrace. Before them on a heap of rags lay the dead body of a child—a tiny child of about three years of age.

It was naked, lying quite straight, so white it was like wax, so thin it was hardly child-like except for its face—a small, peaceful, grave face.

No one spoke for a moment or two. Then Tamara said very softly: "Maman Josef——" The woman lifted her face and looked at the girl. Her face was old, worn and wrung with grief, but tearless.

"Maman Josef," said the girl again, "you must let the men take little Baba now. They must take him to his grave before the guards come round. Mr. Chapek has all made ready."

One of the men in the group bent towards them.

"You must do as Tamara says, Maman Josef," he urged. "If we don't get him away at once they will be here, and then it will be too late. They will throw him in the pit with the others."

"Yes," said another, "you want us to bury him in the quiet corner, don't you? He will be safe there."

"Oh, my Baba—my little, little one!" cried the mother. She tried to wrap the body in an old coat from the heap on which the child was lying, but one of the women took her hands gently away from it.

"Oh God, must he be buried naked then?" wailed the woman, clinging to the coat. "Is there nothing I can wrap him in?"

" No, Maman Josef," said one of the men. " We need the clothes—we are the living. Nothing can be spared for the dead."

Maman Josef's face sank on to her hands, and as her face was covered two of the men at a sign from Tamara quickly took up the dead child and moved away with him. When the woman looked up and saw he was gone she fumbled for a moment wildly in the rags as if she thought the child might be still there.

" He's gone ! He's gone. . . ." She strained to get up, but Tamara and the other woman held her fast. " Naked into the earth—so cold. He will be so cold, my little child. . . ."

Tamara said gently : " No, he will not be cold. The earth is warmer than the bitter winds. Think of him as a little seed, Maman Josef—a little seed in the earth. They grow and flowers come up out of the warm earth. We have seen them even here in the untrodden places."

As she was speaking there was a sudden disturbance at the end of the hut and a number of people appeared. They almost ran into the room, and looked dazed and bewildered, like a herd of cattle. Some were carrying bundles, some had coats huddled about them, many were carrying children or dragging them by the hand as they cried and looked back towards the door.

14

It was a fresh batch of prisoners. They were being thrust forward by the German guards in the rear, one of whom bawled out like a cattle-drover: " Get on, there ! These are your quarters—a bit crowded, but you'll be warmer, crammed together like the swine you are ! "

The other guards laughed and one said : " Yes, and think yourselves lucky that you weren't sent to a warmer place. There's one ready for you not so far away."

There was a deathly silence, even the children were hushed, until the guards withdrew, but immediately they were gone babel broke out. The whole hut, except for the little group round the bereaved woman, gathered about the new-comers. A thousand questions were flung at them in half the tongues of Europe.

" Where are you from ? "

" What camp are you come from ? "

The new arrivals were clutched at, held with frenzied hands. The air throbbed with gesticulation, cries, beseechings. Some looked quite crazed, gibbering with anxiety, terror, hope. All were asking for news of their villages or towns, many for relatives or friends.

" Have you seen my child . . . ? My wife—my father—my mother ? "

Names belonging to many nationalities were shouted, but always the chief question was repeated : " Where are you from?" And the answer was always the same: "From the south."

At last the crowd broke up into small knots of people, and they said to one another: "It is always the same now. They are being moved up north all the time. Soon we shall be moved again."

Some of them turned away to sink down, others to the wall in attitudes of despair.

"Another march. . . ."

"Another hell of travel in cattle-trucks. . . ."

"Another camp—perhaps extermination this time."

One man standing by himself in the middle of the hut suddenly cried out loudly: "Don't you notice one thing? We are being moved north all the time. That means the army is retreating. It can mean nothing else. At any time this camp might be overrun. We might be freed!"

"If they are not too late," said another. "This camp is full to overflowing already. Have you not seen the pile of unburied dead?"

"Yes, that is so," said an old man with a shawl over his head. "But I see another thing also. The guards are fewer. They cannot spare the men to dig the pits, and most of us are too weak to lift a pick or shovel."

"The food is getting less and less," said a woman, so emaciated it seemed incredible that she was capable of any movement or even sound. " Soon they will stop feeding us altogether. Even if the others do come it will be too late for most of us."

The new prisoners were trying to find a few feet of floor space for themselves and their wretched bundles. There was some scuffling and squabbling over this in a weak, lethargic sort of way. They were a mixed lot, impossible to pick out class or race ; all were dirty, dishevelled and grey with fatigue. Some were in prison garb, others still in the clothing they had been wearing when captured. These did not look quite so thin as those in prison dress.

One in particular, a young lad of about seventeen or eighteen, was wearing very ragged corduroy velveteen trousers and the remnants of a jacket over a grey plaid shirt. He was a black-haired boy with large dark eyes that stared about almost madly. He looked, and was, a gipsy. He was like a captured beast. He walked round and round the hut just as a newly caged fox might have done, completely regardless of the others. Round and round the walls he went, looking at the small high windows, stepping over the recumbent figures on the floor, ignoring everything in his path and blind to everything but the windows. His face was a concentrated mask of agonized longing for escape.

Nobody seemed to take any notice of him; he was entirely without family or belongings. Yet there was one person in the crowded place watching him; it was Tamara, still crouched by Maman Josef. She watched him, her eyes moving round with him in his endless traversing of the hut. And her eyes were filled with an infinite pity.

It was night in the hut now. All was dark except for a beam of light that came through the windows at regular intervals. This was the light from the search-light of the watch-tower that perpetually ringed the wire enclosure with its beam in case any desperate wretch might make his pitiful effort to escape, when a few shots would ring out, a shout or two or a scream, and another body would be added to the pile by the pits.

In the intermittent glow of the searchlight could be seen the huddled mass of sleepers in the hut, an indiscriminate huddle of shapes in a miasma of stench.

Faces glimmered in the light. First Maman Josef. Her face was cadaverous; great shadows round the eyes and under the cheekbones. The eyes were closed, the lips tightly sealed. Her hands were held up closely under her face. They were clasping a cross. It was only two sticks roughly tied together, but her hands grasped it as a drowning man grasps a rope—so tightly that the light glistened on the bony knuckles.

Another face was Tamara's. She was lying on her back, her face turned up to the roof of the hut. Her eyes were widely opened. Presently she raised her head a little and stayed thus a moment, listening.

There was the face of the young gipsy boy. This one was puffy and swollen with weeping. It was a very young face, and with the tears that glistened on it and the rumpled hair shaken over the eyes, it looked almost that of a child. But the despair in it was not that of a homesick child; it had an agony written on it too deep for that.

After listening for a while, Tamara got up from her place by the side of Maman Josef and crawled with infinite care among the stinking heaps of rags to where the boy was lying. She laid her hand on his head.

He looked up startled with a gasp of horror. The light illuminated her face for a second as she looked down at him. It was very gentle.

"Poor boy," she said, in a whisper. "Don't cry. It only wastes your strength and you have need of it. You have not been a prisoner long?"

He stared up at her, holding his breath.

"Not long . . . at least I don't know. I forget," he whispered at last. "I don't know anything any more. Only that I must get out . . . I must get out!"

His voice rose a little, harsh with a rising hysteria, and Tamara put her hand over his mouth.

"No, you mustn't think of that," she told him; "you must never think of that. It is no good. Many have tried and all are dead—shot or killed on the wire. If you try we all suffer—if one can suffer any more; some of us are beyond it, I think. I have been in these places a long time. I know how it is. The only thing to do is to endure—*everything*."

"Is there no hope, then?" he asked her.

"I used to think there was no hope," said Tamara, "but just lately some of us think there may be yet a little hope." She turned to go. "Sleep now," she said softly. "We can still escape in sleep. . . ."

The boy put out a hand and grasped her sleeve.

"Don't go—don't leave me. Don't go!"

"I must," she said, removing his burning fingers one by one from their hold on her arm. "Tomorrow I will see you again and we'll talk then. Don't resist anything, or say anything, or show any feeling for anything, no matter what you see or hear. Now sleep and don't weep any more."

She crawled back to her place by the side of Maman Josef, who lay as still as a stone.

The hut was full of noises; of little sighs, of moans and stifled cries. At the far end of the room from a corner came the sound of a baby's crying. Thin and weak, a thread of sound on and on in the darkness. Outside the wind played with a small piece of black rag that was caught on a bit of guttering on a corner of the hut. It fluttered and flapped like a sentient thing and seemed to be trying to get free and fly into the black windy sky. The wind sang to it—an old weary song, thin and thready as the baby's cry—a song of all the sorrows of Europe: of the persecutions, the desolation of mankind; of sins and despairs; of the Black Death and of plagues and wars and famines . . . a little sinister wind singing of the white cold of Nature and the black cold of men's hearts.

II

Tamara and Jean, the young gipsy lad, were sitting under the pine trees on the little knoll where Tamara used to sit alone watching for the wild swans. There was silence between them. The boy sat with his head hanging in an attitude of dejection. Tamara lay back weakly against the red-brown bole of the tree, but her face was upturned as usual, watching the sky.

"I think they may come again tonight," she said, half to herself. "The sky is clear and we should see them if they come, Jean."

The boy did not stir. After a bit he said: "I don't believe they ever come. I don't believe there can be anything alive in this dreadful place—nor anywhere near it. Not in the whole country."

Tamara did not reply but turned her head and looked at him.

"Jean," she said suddenly, "where do you come from? Do you remember?"

Still without looking up, he shook his head.

"I don't know where I was born," he said. "People like us don't have houses. We had a van. We moved to where we wanted to be whenever we wanted to. We went to fairs, mostly in the little towns. Sometimes we went with circuses. My mother made brushes and flowers out of wood shavings, and my father—— Oh, Mother! Oh, Father! . . ." Suddenly his face was convulsed. He put his hand over his eyes.

"I lived in a van too," said Tamara dreamily. "There were many of us. We had a camp when I was little. I remember the fires and the cooking-pots and the music at night. We danced. We were gay and happy. Then one night the soldiers came on us quite suddenly. They rounded us all up and burnt the vans and scattered the camp. A lot of us were killed, I think—we all got separated in the terror. Some tried to run away. I can't remember much—only long long journeys in terrible cold. People died all the way. We got somewhere and then somewhere else. I lost my father and my mother and sisters. I don't know where they are. I know I have been in prison a very long time, but I don't know how long. There is no way of telling."

The boy turned to face her, brushing the long hair away from his eyes.

"Tamara—why am *I* put in prison?" he asked. "I can't understand it. Do you think it is because I stole some chickens from a farmer the night before the soldiers came? Did they think we were thieves? Tamara—will they kill us, do you think?"

"I don't know," she said. "They might, or we might just die. No one knows. They do kill the Jews and us too—at least they say so in the camps. At any rate people are taken away in batches and nobody ever sees them again."

He stared at her.

"But why? Why? I don't understand. What have we done wrong?"

"I think that the Jews did something very bad a long time ago," she answered him after a pause for consideration; her small face took on a curiously ancient and wise expression as she spoke. "For us, I don't think it's that. I think it is just because we were free and had no places to stop in—and that is not allowed any more."

Jean moved restlessly and struggled to his knees. He twisted his hands together and stared out beyond the wire to the dark, distant country.

"Oh, Tamara," he cried desperately, "can't we get out? Can't we get away? I know the direction we should go if only we can get out!"

"How do you know?" Tamara looked at him curiously.

"By the stars at night. We should go south—over there." He pointed in the direction of the lake.

"That is the way the swans go," said the girl. "And now is about the time of their coming. Let's keep still and watch now. Don't talk any more—it only makes us sad."

They were silent again, watching the sky once more. Presently, sure enough, the swans appeared, flying high, swiftly, with their purposeful, strong flight.

"There, you see . . . !" said Tamara, and the faintest flush of pleasure came for a second to her pale cheeks.

Jean's face was rapt, ecstatic.

"They are free!" he cried. "Oh, Tamara, if ever we escape we must never never never be caught again! We must always hide for ever afterwards. Oh God, if we could only *get out—get out*!"

Tamara reached up and put her hand on his arm, her enormous eyes filled with tears.

"Don't, Jean. It's no good. We must be humble—never resist. We must just try to live till the end. They *will* kill you if you resist." She paused a moment and her eyes wandered to the now far-distant swans, a white line gleaming against the heavy grey sky. "Do you know what I feel?" she went on. "I feel that so long as the swans fly over there is hope for us. Try to think that too."

25

She got to her feet, slowly and laboriously as might an aged person.

"Now we must go back to the others. It is always safer to keep with the others and try not to be noticed. The guard is not so bad as it was, but they are still always on the watch, and one never knows what they are thinking or planning to do to us."

The hut was a scene of the wildest confusion. People were gathering their wretched belongings and baggage as best they could amid a babel of cries and shouts. Women were crying, children wailing; the noise was like that of a frightened herd and the stench was indescribable as they struggled and huddled and feebly pushed. Some collapsed, to be dragged up again by a distracted relative. A German guard at the door was bawling: "All out! All out! Clear the hut. All out and muster on the square. The camp is being evacuated."

More soldiers began pushing their way through to the back of the seething crowd to kick and belabour those in the rear, to hasten the poor creatures towards the door.

The square was a barren patch of ground surrounded on three sides by huts, out of which poured more prisoners to swell the crowd already gathered outside. The fourth side opened on to a wide road which led to the main prison gates, which were open and guarded by soldiers with machine-guns and bayonets. All round the milling mass of people were more soldiers and guards. These, with rifle butt, truncheon and boot, were mustering the throng into some semblance of lines. Old people fell and were kicked up again or lay where they fell, to be trampled upon by the terrified herd. Children screamed and shrieks rang out here and there, and above the tumult could be heard the bawled-out orders of the guard. It was a scene of hideous violence and brutality.

There were but three questions in the hearts of every one of the prisoners: "Where to this time? Is this the end? Is it to be on foot or in the open cattle-wagons again? Where now? Where now?"

Then suddenly the soldiers on guard at the prison gates could be seen gesticulating and pointing. The warders on the watch-towers began yelling something through megaphones, and a rattle of machine-gun fire began from several points. Shooting back over their shoulders down the road, the soldiers began to run from the gates.

Confusion broke out anew in the square, and some of the prisoners started to rush towards the now unguarded gates. Shot down by the soldiers in the square before they reached them, most of them fell, but they were followed by a wave of others. The shooting became sporadic and died down and a great shout went up.

27

"The British ! It is the British !"

Armoured cars appeared in the road, and men in khaki uniforms ran towards the camp ; others followed from huge lorries, to be immediately surrounded by the frantic prisoners—swallowed up by clutching hands.

It was impossible to gain order ; pandemonium reigned, and many of the prisoners were now out in the road—outside the barbed wire of their prison for the first time in years.

Struggling in the crush were Tamara and Jean. Jean had hold of the girl with both hands to save her from being flung down, and they were jostled and thrust out into the road by the uncontrollable crowd and into the field on its other side.

At last they were on the outskirts of the mob. Tamara was dazed and clung to Jean with her eyes tightly shut, dizzy and swaying, but Jean looked about him wildly in all directions.

"Tamara," he shouted into her ear, "now is our chance ! We can get away ! That wood over there . . . it's quite close. Do you think you can reach it ? Oh, be quick—hurry ! Come now—quick—*quick* !"

He began to drag her along towards a strip of woodland. It was only about a couple of hundred yards away, but she was so weak with starvation and terror that she was unable to do more than totter. She tried to gasp out to Jean that the British soldiers had come to set them free, but he would take no notice of her and struggled on, half carrying, half dragging her.

They reached the first thin covering of trees. Fearfully he looked back. No one seemed to have seen their flight. The column of British soldiers were now wholly concerned with trying to control the frenzied prisoners who were besieging them and surrounding the cars and lorries, trying to climb into them, pushing the children aboard. He struggled on with Tamara, deeper into the wood, panting and sweating, on and on—a new strength rising from his desperation.

By now the wood was really thick, with a dense undergrowth. Plunging, half falling, he fought his way in until he could go no farther, and at length fell with Tamara half under him. Exhausted, they lay without moving for some time.

When he had recovered himself a little Jean lifted his head to listen. There was no sound to be heard now but the soft hush of the trees above them. Tamara opened her eyes slowly, like someone awakening from a deep sleep. Jean whispered: "We are free. We got away. Do you understand, Tamara? We will never be caught again."

"Never—be—caught—again. . . ." Her answer was like a sigh. Her eyes closed again and Jean's head fell back on to the earth; it smelt sweet and was cool to his burning face. Sleep came down on them like a curtain and they slept from sheer exhaustion, without even altering their positions.

Some hours later they roused and sat upright. It was about the hour of sunset and so silent in the wood that they might have been a hundred miles from the scenes of war and the horrors of the concentration camp. High above them the trees rocked gently against the darkening sky where a few faint stars were beginning to appear. It was very cold, and Tamara was shivering. Jean took her icy hands into his.

" Do you think you can walk any farther ? " he asked her. " I think we should try and get farther away from the camp and the soldiers before it is quite dark. They may try to look for us. See if you can stand."

The girl made an effort, got to her feet, but sank down again.

" Oh, Jean," she moaned, " I can't—I can't go farther. You must go on without me. You must go, but I had better go back to the camp. The British soldiers will treat us well, I think. They *couldn't* want to kill us. They'll give us food. We haven't any food here, Jean—and no water. Don't you think we had both better return ? "

He shook his head violently.

" No—no, Tamara ! They will imprison us again—I'm sure they will. I don't trust them, I shall never trust anyone again. No, we must go on—we'll hide

by day and travel by night. I'll get food for you—
we'll manage, you'll see. Stay with me." He shook her
passionately. "Please stay! I'll find some way of
getting us into a country we know and where we can
be really free, if only you will trust me. Don't leave
me. . . ."

Tamara made no answer. He looked at her, wondering if she could have fallen asleep again; then
closer, with a sudden fear that she might be dead, but
she turned her head a little and smiled at him.

"Look," he said, "if you cannot move I will build
a little tent of wood and leaves for you here, and you
must lie close as a sitting partridge while I creep out
and see if I can find anything we can eat."

"How would you find me again?" she whispered.

"Oh, I'd find you. I've not forgotten how to find
my way in a forest. Only trust me, Tamara—I'll find
something for us to eat somehow now we are out of
that awful place."

"You might be shot and I should never know."

"They won't see me," he assured her boldly. "The
dusk is a good time; I shall move like a fox. That's
it, Tamara—we must live like foxes."

While he was talking and trying to soothe and re-
assure her he was silently collecting sticks and branches
and making a little erection with them like a bivouac
tent. He stuck ferns and brushwood upright between

the sticks until there was a thick layer of protection, indistinguishable in the dim light from the rest of the undergrowth. When it was finished the girl crept inside. Jean was gone, as silently as a shadow.

It was quite dark when he returned, a darker blur in the faint starlight.

"Tamara?" he whispered. There was a rustle and her face appeared through the branches.

"Oh, Jean—Jean, how wonderful to see you. I was afraid you were not coming back. Oh, Jean—water! Have you got some water?"

"Yes. Let me creep inside. Let's lie with our heads outside; we can see enough for me to show you what I have found." He wormed his way in beside her. "There now!" He produced a soldier's army water-bottle, unscrewed it and held it to her lips. She tried to drink it greedily, but Jean said "No", and would only allow her a small amount. He took a little himself, then laid the bottle aside.

"Now, here is some food." He twisted round, reaching into his pockets, pulling out about half a loaf of white bread, from which he broke a little piece for each. They ate like wolves. Tamara gazed in wonder at the bread.

"What kind of food is it?" she asked, forgetting for the moment the taste of white bread. "Is it cake?"

" No, of course not." He looked at her scornfully.
" It's bread, of course. We mustn't eat any more of it
now. I've got some white sweets—look. I've already
eaten one—they're sweet and taste like milk."

He produced a tin of Horlicks Malted Milk tablets
and gave her one. Tamara put it in her mouth.

" Oh, Jean ! " she gasped, like a surprised child ; but
she did not smile or laugh, she was just gravely astonished.

"And that's not all," said Jean proudly. " Look—a
knife ! A beauty."

He showed her a soldier's sheath-knife, turning it
over and over in his dark hands and feeling the edge
and the point with pleased satisfaction.

"And that's not all," fishing a petrol lighter out of
his pocket.

" What is that ? " she asked.

" It's a lighter. Better than matches. You rub a
little wheel and it makes a spark and then a flame. They
used to sell them at the fairs. And last of all this.
Wait. . . ."

With a good deal of wriggling he managed to pull
out from under his coat a quite large bundle of clothing.
It was a pair of soldier's trousers and a cape. He shook
them out."

" You must take off that dress and put these on
instead," he told her. "Anyone could see you in that
dress and know where you came from. These are the

colour of the earth; you won't be so easily seen in them, and you'll be warmer."

" Oh, Jean, you are wonderful—how can I thank you ? "

" Put them on now," he commanded.

Tamara crawled out from the wigwam-like tent, and Jean followed her, to hold her while she took off her striped prison dress. It took some time to do this, for her movements were slow and weak, but at last it was off. For a moment her thin body gleamed white in the starlight. With his help she pulled on the trousers; he tied them round her waist with a strip torn off the discarded dress. Then he wrapped the cape around her. She peered down at the trousers and felt them with her fingers.

" Jean, there is a dark stiff patch on the trousers. What is it ? "

" It's blood," he said briefly. " We can wash it off at the first stream we come to."

She was silent a minute, still fingering the clothes.

" Jean, where did you get all these things ? " she whispered. " Was it from a dead man ? "

" Yes. I found him in a ditch—at the end of the wood. He hadn't been killed very long."

" Did . . . did you see his face ? "

" Yes. He was young, like me. A British soldier. Why do you want to know ? "

"I don't know," she sighed. "I just wondered what he looked like."

"Well, I don't think it matters," said Jean, beginning to crawl back into the branches of the tent and making room for the girl. "Come on, get in. We must sleep and lie here all day; not move or make a sound until tomorrow night. You'll be stronger after the food and rest. Then we shall start to travel south. We shall travel like foxes, creeping along the hedges and ditches, through woods. Never near roads. And we must listen and listen and watch all the way. Are you warmer? Go to sleep now and don't talk any more."

They slept while the night wore itself out and the stars faded as the grey dawn broke. They slept when the pale sun came up and the first tiny rustlings and movements of bird and beast broke the silence of the night. They slept at intervals all through the day, waking now and then to eat a little, or drink, and to listen intently for any sounds that might signify the approach of man. At last, at dusk the following night, they crept out of their hiding-place, stiff and chilly, for Jean now considered it was time for them to begin their long journey south—to freedom.

III

At first Tamara was so weak she could not do more than a few miles a day, hobbling slowly with the help of Jean and a stout stick he cut for her from a hazel. At the beginning he was a little impatient with her, as he, not having been imprisoned long, was not so weak and starved as she; he was anxious to get on—to get farther—to put as many miles as they could between themselves and the dreadful camp, the thought of which made him sweat with fear. But he soon saw that she did not lack courage, and that it was useless and cruel to urge her to do more than she could.

Having been used to very little to eat for so long, they found that they could only eat quite a small amount each day, and that helped to spin their meagre rations out for a time. However, the little they did eat began quite soon to manifest itself in increased strength.

Both being of gipsy stock, they were naturally strong and healthy. Jean was an expert thief. He knew how to move like a cat, and at each dawn, after finding a hiding-place for the girl, he would creep forth by himself, foraging for food and exploring the country, climbing up tall trees to get a bird's-eye view of the country for the next day's travel, and to try and ascertain if there were any troops or men in the locality.

He never came back empty-handed from these forays. The part of the country they passed through had been largely untouched by war. Whole villages often seemed to be intact, though here and there they would come upon burned-out farms and houses and blasted villages. Jean would creep up to the inhabited farms, get into the cow byres to milk one of the cows into a can he had picked up. He took pleasure in the warmth of the presence of the quiet beasts in the dim light of the chill dawns. They took no more notice of him than if he had been the farm cat or one of the great owls that roosted in the rafters of their sheds.

He was often tempted to try and steal eggs, but dared not risk the noise of frightened hens rousing the peasants. Once he found a nest full of hen's eggs in the side of a haystack, glimmering whitely, fragile as pearls in the wan light. He came upon stores of apples, and of course onions and turnips and potatoes. His nose was so keen that he could smell them out from a considerable distance. Such things as these they lived on, and drank water from the streams and ponds, where sometimes they found cresses. They dared not try to cook anything for fear the gleam of a fire might be seen or a rising plume of smoke.

They avoided all the roads; they could often hear great columns of heavy traffic moving along them through the nights. Aeroplanes continually roared overhead, but the bombs and the gunfire, the flashes and fires they had become so used to seeing no longer seemed to be there.

In spite of the boy's care and infinite caution, they were several times near discovery by small posses of soldiers, who once or twice came so perilously near them that Jean and Tamara could actually hear their speech. But it was never in a language they recognized.

Jean's hearing and sense of smell were as acute as an animal's, and his use for all kinds of cover as wily as a fox's. Thick ivy, trees, scrub, ditch bottoms, ferns, even rough grass came to their aid; and as they travelled they became always more earth-stained, so that the earth seemed to take them to itself and protect them as it does the sitting partridge, the wild hare, and all its other children. It also nurtured that strange, ever new flame of life in them as the mysterious light of early spring wakes the dormant seed, the waiting root, patient under the chill soil, and stirs the blood of bird and beast.

The weather was kind to them, warmer, and there were not many nights without stars to help them on their journey southwards. But, being near blossom time, they had not the advantage of wild fruit, and Jean would sometimes curse the dawn chorus of birds which prevented him from hearing the other sounds he was perpetually listening for—the sound of mankind or prowling dog.

Dogs were a real danger, for some of the farm dogs were as large and savage as wolves, which many of them resembled. They had often to make wide detours to avoid villages and farms as well as the small towns—and not infrequently the camps of soldiers— and the lengthening days and shorter nights made it doubly imperative to find adequate hiding-places before nightfall.

Tamara was gradually growing stronger and beginning to look the graceful gipsy girl that she naturally was. The bloom of youth returned to her face, her cheeks to take on the golden-red downiness of a peach ; and though she was still habitually grave and anxious, her fears were slowly slipping from her. They were both dirty and ragged, but it was with the clean dirt of earth and the green mould of the trees they so intimately lived with—not the filth of a concentration camp.

Jean's hair grew long, black and wild, almost to his shoulders, until he could bear it no longer and begged Tamara to try and cut it shorter with the sheath-knife, which he had sharpened almost to razor keenness. She tried, but the effect was as ludicrous as the grimaces he made as she sawed at his hair, and she flung down the knife and burst into a peal of laughter. He jumped up from the tree-stump on which he had been seated for the operation.

"Tamara," he cried, "you laughed! This is the very first time you have laughed—d'you know that?"

Half scowling, half laughing himself, he made a dive at her. She avoided him and began to run, still laughing and looking back at him through her hair. She was not strong enough or swift enough to get far before he caught her. She struggled in his grasp, swayed, tottered and fell with the boy on top of her. They lay panting for a second; then as she heaved and squirmed beneath him he suddenly began to kiss her. He rained hot boyish kisses on her mouth, her cheeks, her neck as she lay quite still now with astonishment. When his hands began to wander over her body she moved again and and pushed him away. He released her abruptly and they got to their feet. Both stared at one another, the laughter gone from their faces. They were like two children who have suddenly discovered a strange secret. Then each turned away, and Jean soon began to resume his customary manner of slightly scornful protectiveness.

But Tamara's manner had undergone a change. She watched Jean now out of the corner of her eye, and when she thought he wasn't looking at her. Her expression was one of gentle wonder.

Nothing was said between them of the incident. Jean maintained his lordly attitude towards her by day; but in the nights, when they lay huddled together for warmth under a hedge or in some branchy thicket, she would often rouse dreamily out of sleep to feel his hands moving about her body, caressing her small, still child-like breasts and her long slender thighs, and she would lie, still in the grey twilight of half-sleep, soothed and yet strangely stirred by the softly moving hands.

One morning, as they ate their breakfast of a bit of very dry bread and a slice of turnip and drank some milk out of the tin can, she announced : " Jean, I think we should get married."

He glanced at her quickly, surprised, and then looked away. There was a long silence; he began digging a hole in the soft black soil of the wood they were sitting in.

" Well . . . I don't mind," he said at last, and then added under his breath, " but I think it's silly."

"It's not silly," said Tamara with some indignation in her voice. "It's the thing to do."

"Well—how can we get married?" he asked, gruffly. "There's nobody here to marry us."

Tamara was silent. This was something she had not considered. She sat thoughtfully for a while, her hands clasped round her knees, her long black hair falling round her face.

"How did *your* people get married?" she asked at length.

"Oh, there was a feast and music and dancing—and a great fire in the middle. The man and the woman held hands and jumped over the fire. Then the king of the camp said they were man and wife. And all the men got drunk."

Tamara sighed.

"We can't light a fire, I suppose?" she asked doubtfully.

"No—too dangerous. It might be seen."

They lapsed into silence again. Jean shot a quick glance at Tamara.

"Well, what d'you suggest we do?" he asked, beginning to be a little interested in spite of himself, now that the first shock of the proposal was over.

"I remember my mother telling me that in her tribe in the old days the people who wanted to get married would go to a little stream, and one would stand on one side and one on the other. Then they would kneel down and clasp hands under the water and would make a vow to be true to each other—for ever," said Tamara, her eyes following a pigeon that had just flown into a tree overhead and was now perched on the swaying branch turning its head from side to side and watching them. "And that would be a true marriage," she added.

Jean nodded.

"Well, that's easy," he said. "There's a stream in this wood; I got water from it just now."

She got up and pulled Jean to his feet. He led her through the trees for a while until they came upon a small brown stream that curved its way through a thicket of hazel bushes and ferns. It had dug itself a deep bed between banks, but they followed its course until they found a place where it had narrowed into a bright swift rivulet, flowing over small stones.

"This should do," said Tamara, looking at it critically. "You get over the other side and see if you can reach my hand."

They knelt down on the silvery shingle, leant towards each other and clasped hands under the clear water.

"Don't pull or you'll have me in," cried Jean, who was inclined to laugh. But Tamara was grave, her face solemn and intent.

"Now you must say: 'I, Jean, promise to be true to thee, Tamara, until death,'" she told him.

"I, Jean, promise to be true to thee, Tamara, until death," he repeated obediently.

"I, Tamara, promise to be true to thee, Jean, until death," said Tamara. He continued to hold her hand beneath the water, looking at her inquiringly.

"That's all," she said simply, and they got to their feet. Jean wiped his hand slightly shamefacedly on the seat of his trousers, and without speaking again they went back to their encampment under the oak tree, Jean whistling and slightly in the lead, as befitted a man with a wife.

They waited in the wood all day, and at moonrise resumed their journey.

IV

Daily Tamara grew stronger and more active. As time passed and their fears lessened Jean developed more and more as an expert thief. He would creep up to the very windows of houses at night, and frequently a farmer's wife's clothes-line would be short of a garment or two if she had been careless enough to leave them out overnight. He would listen at the windows for voices talking within, hoping to discover what country they were in. But so far he had not been able to understand anything he had overheard from the lighted windows against which he crouched.

"We haven't got there yet," he would say to Tamara. "When I hear French spoken I shall know we are *nearly* safe at any rate. We must keep on."

And on they went. The moon had waned and waxed again, and many were the sights they saw in their strange journey by its weird, soft light. They moved across old battlegrounds—hideously blasted areas, cratered like the moon itself, full of contorted shapes of unnameable machines, shattered guns and spiky, grotesque trees. Sometimes the ground would be burnt for considerable distances, and they would emerge from it blackened and dusty as sweeps.

Now and then they came upon great aeroplanes lying shattered and broken, like gigantic silvery birds in the broken glades of the woods. Often more gruesome objects would manifest themselves in the shape of a huddled mass of clothing and a hideous odour. Once they saw a dead airman hanging head downwards from a tree, his parachute feebly stirring in the wind on the ground below him like a still living thing.

Their strangest encounter took place one night when Jean's sharp ears heard an inexplicable sound; the roaring of a wild beast from somewhere not far away from them. Tamara was frightened and clutched Jean's arm. As if turned to stone, they stood to listen. At first they believed it to be a bull or a stag, or even a wild boar. After a while curiosity impelled them to go cautiously a little farther, when they saw a small

46

farmstead set at the end of a big field. They crept
closer, skirting the farm, to find behind it in another
field a great cluster of vans. From one of these vans
the roaring came once more, terrifying and barbaric in
that pastoral setting—a jungle sound.

"Tamara," exclaimed Jean in a whisper, "I know
what it is—I've seen vans like that before. It's a travelling
menagerie—part of a circus perhaps. There's a tiger
in one of those vans. Oh, I must go and see ! We must
get closer . . . will you wait for me ? "

" No." Tamara shook her head. " I'll come with
you—but there may be dogs. . . ."

" They will soon hear us if there are any. We could
get away to that belt of trees if anyone gives the
alarm," he assured her urgently. " Come on—I want
to see it."

Hand in hand they stole forward. There in the
moonlight they found a stranded fair with swingboats
and merry-go-rounds, all with their great dragons and
horses glimmering in the moonlight like strange beasts
from the Apocalypse. Huge stacks of equipment,
mysterious tarpaulin-covered objects, caravans, loomed
up all round, and the great animal vans, from which
the sounds of thuds and grunts told of the restless
inmates within. Every now and then the imprisoned
tiger raised his voice to shatter the very stars with his
useless rage.

47

In one corner they came upon a tethered elephant, huge, grey and immobile.

At last Tamara, saddened by the barred vans and the sense of imprisonment, begged Jean to come away. Her heart was beating like a tiny bird in her throat, an old fear renewed itself and her eyes glistened with tears. Reluctantly Jean turned away.

As they moved silently across the misty fields they came upon some of the circus horses, turned out to grass —beautiful white creatures, a little shaggy with their winter coats still upon them, they had long manes and tails almost to the ground. Jean was entranced. Being a gipsy boy, he had a love of horses bred in him for generations back, an ineradicable streak. He could not resist going to them. They flung up their heads and snorted at his approach. Tamara held her breath lest they should stampede in sudden fright and arouse the sleeping camp. But no, they seemed to recognize the gipsy as he spoke to them in some strange soft language of his own, and came across the field to him with pricked ears and answering soft whinneyings. They came close, smelling his hands and his clothes—a strange group in the moonlight, the wild dark boy and the great white horses.

One morning after one of his dawn forays Jean returned to her in a state of some excitement to tell her that on listening outside a lonely cottage with a lighted upstairs window he had heard the voice of a woman singing to a child.

"She was singing a song I knew," he told her. "She was singing in French——" He sang a few bars of a simple country song. "Like that," he said.

"Oh, Jean!" Tamara gazed at the boy with wide-open eyes. "Could it mean that we are nearly safe?"

"We can't be sure yet. Wait until we try the next village; we will both listen there if you're brave enough, and if we hear French being spoken in several houses we shall know we are on the border." His eyes gleamed with excitement, then he added: "But we shall have to be even more careful, for the borders are sure to have guards covering every inch of the ground."

At the mention of guards and the thought of fresh dangers to be faced, for she had begun to feel secure in the loneliness of the forests and the wilder country they had been passing through, Tamara began to tremble. Her legs shook and she sank to the ground, staring about her with great fear-darkened eyes like a hare until Jean was forced to take her in his arms.

"Don't be afraid," he said. "Surely you can trust me?" And with boyish boastfulness: "Surely you've seen how clever I am? I have got us both all this way. I shall get us into France, never you fear!"

He spent some hours in the early light of the following

morning surveying the lie of the land from the top-most branches of a tall tree, and discovered that a road-way running across their course south showed unmis-takable signs of being patrolled.

It did not seem to be a main thoroughfare, but at frequent intervals soldiers on motorcycles passed up and down it with rifles slung on their shoulders. They were riding slowly and appeared to be keeping a watchful eye on the country surrounding the road. About here, unfortunately, the country was bare of cover, but he saw there was a small willow-edged river that wound through the fields under deep overhanging banks. It passed under the road by way of a little bridge. He decided at length that this would be the only way of getting across the boundary road, if that was what it was. Whatever it was, there seemed to be too much traffic on it for it to be safe for them to make a dash to safety overland.

That same evening they retraced their steps about half a mile and joined the small river some distance from the bridge. They waded in and found the water was fairly shallow—not more than waist deep in most places.

"If, when we get to the bridge," he told Tamara, "a soldier or anyone should be on the road, we must duck down under the water like a waterhen with only our noses out and wait until they have passed. And at all costs we must not splash or stumble. Go very slowly and take hold of my coat. We shall have to go a long way in the water, but it is the only way, so take care."

They crept along, close under the bank, Jean feeling his way before them with a long stick, crouching under overhanging brambles which caught their hair and clung to their clothes with fiendish tenacity. It was hard work, and every now and then they were forced to stop to gain breath. The water was cold and Tamara began to feel her legs getting numb.

At last the bridge was reached. The water here was deep, and they were halfway through when suddenly they heard a motorcycle slowly—too slowly—approaching. They stopped and listened, holding their breath. Surely he would pass over? But no, just before he got to the bridge they heard the engine splutter and stop. Had he seen them? They sank down in the water up to their necks. Jean stared up at the dark arch of the bridge above them with its dripping green weeds and small grey stalactites, on each of which hung a tiny drop of quivering water.

" Pull your hair over your face," he hissed to Tamara ; " we shall look like weedy stones. He may not see us even if he looks over the edge."

A moment of desperate suspense passed, then they heard the engine being revved up to start again ; another moment and it had passed over their heads and they heard it fade away into the distance.

"Quick, now—quick, before another comes!" gasped Jean. Shivering and with water pouring from their hair and clothes, they crept out of the tunnel and gained the shadow of the bank on the other side.

There the willows were thick enough and the water sufficiently shallow for them to get along at a better speed, and they continued thus in the water for nearly another half-mile until the girl was so exhausted that Jean could see that she could go no farther. Her teeth were rattling in her head, her face was as white as the little crowns of froth that eddied round and round in the backwaters under the banks.

Jean pulled himself out of the water and peered with infinite caution over the top of the bank. He saw they were still in somewhat bare country, but that a line of hedgerow led to a patch of willow scrub not far away. This would have to do, and he dragged her out. They set out once more, half crawling along the hedge bottom.

It was by now well on into the morning, with the sun up and shining with the cold brilliance of early spring. Jean prayed that no peasant workmen or prowling dog would come that way.

At the end of the hedge they found a small raised bit of ground in the centre of the scrub; it was quite dry and surrounded by reeds. A wild duck flew up with a clatter of wings which paralysed them both for a minute until silence ensued, broken only by the rustling of the dry yellow reeds and rushes. They took off their dripping garments and wrung them out and lay down on the dry reed-bed for the sun to warm their shivering bodies. Jean rubbed Tamara until at last she began to get some feeling of life back into her numbed limbs. Huddled up together, with the sun pouring down a merciful warmth, and lulled by the endless whispering conversation of the reeds, they fell asleep.

After that adventure they continued their journey south without much incident, except that the weather took a dramatic turn. The wind that had been soft and almost balmy lashed itself into a gale. The trees under which they sheltered at night rocked and groaned and crashed their branches together over their heads, roared in the streaming wind and in the blackness which made it impossible for them to travel by night. It blew up huge dark clouds that raced over the landscape. Then rain came, sweeping like great shadowy ghosts across the land, which became grey and sodden. The ditch bottoms were soon waterlogged, and Tamara and Jean were forced to find shelter in a small, tumbledown shed in a field—too close for their peace of mind to a farmstead they knew to be inhabited. But after three days and nights the weather cleared, the sun came out again fitfully, and at nightfall stars showed once more between the ragged drifts of scud so that they were able to proceed again on their way.

Now, and with renewed hope, they listened whenever they could to any speech of the women in the houses or men in the fields. Once they heard a ploughman shouting to his team in French, and soon all the talk they overheard in farms and cottages, the shrill conversation of children at play in distant village streets, was in the language they knew.

" We are in France," said Jean to Tamara.

All the same, they went on hiding by day and travelling by night, until one day he told Tamara that he felt sure they were drawing near to a forest. He had climbed the tallest tree he could find, and as far as he could see there seemed to be nothing before him but forest to horizon's farthest rim. A great dark, mysterious mass rising from a stretch of heathy land covered with gorse bushes and heather.

"There we shall be safe ! " he said joyfully. " We'll build ourselves a proper camp in the forest. I will hunt and you shall cook. We shall be able to make a fire and live like a king and queen."

V

The forest was very beautiful. The trees were mixed oak and beech, with long belts and groups of dark pines in which the wind perpetually murmured like the sound of a distant sea. Here and there it opened into wide ferny glades and was crisscrossed by grass rides about the width of a small roadway. Occasionally Tamara and Jean would come across metalled roads as well as narrow mossy lanes. There was little sign of any human being, though once or twice they came across a woodman's or keeper's hut, and once the evidence of a charcoal-burner's camp.

They travelled by day now and had penetrated well into the forest when Jean's acute sense of smell told him they were nearing a village; a warm smell had drifted to his nostrils above the tangy scent of the forest—a smell of smoke, of farm animals, the smell of houses whose open doors let out the emanations of cooking, of clothing, of people. Presently the trees began to thin out and they saw smoke rising into the sky.

Jean made Tamara wait while he went forward to investigate.

Moving silently as a cat he soon came to fields, and in the midst of them, in a slight hollow, there was a small village surrounding an old grey church. The village had an air of almost legendary antiquity; it looked as if it had been dropped in the forest long long ago by some magician and then forever after forgotten. Roads led to it, wandered through it and out into the forest on its farther side.

When he returned Tamara saw that he was smiling; his white teeth flashed in his brown face as he ran towards her.

" We'll stay here," he announced as soon as he was within earshot. " When night comes—or, perhaps better still, in the very early morning when we can see— we'll explore that village and see if we can find food. And you shall come with me this time, for we can easily get away into the trees again if anyone should hear us."

56

They roused at dawn to the chorus of birds—a chorus now pierced by the thin clear crowing of cocks from the village. A new sound this; it came to Jean like a challenge.

"Now," he said to Tamara, "we shall see!"

The sleeping village, that looked as if it were wrapped in a dream so old that nothing would have aroused it anyhow, allowed itself to be explored. No one looked out at them from its tight-shut and curtained windows; nothing moved but one old black-and-white cat busy mousing amongst the crooked gravestones of the churchyard under the black cypresses.

They discovered that the village consisted of about forty cottages, an inn, two little shops and one or two small farmsteads with cow-byres and pigsties. They did not stay long, for it was rapidly growing light; the grey of the dawn sky was slowly taking on a blush of red, but they did not return to their lair empty-handed.

Later that morning Madame Joliot of the inn was astonished to find that two loaves of bread and a piece of cheese were missing from her larder, and soundly scolded her son for a supposed midnight foray on his part. This he strongly denied, but got a good clip over the ear all the same. Madame Joliot, had she known it, was not the only one with something mysteriously missing; the old carpenter, too, found a string of onions and a quantity of apples gone from his out-house. One farmer at least was surprised at the small yield of milk from his cows that morning.

" We will stay here—for a time, anyhow," said Jean. " I'm going to make a camp deep in the woods where we can build a fire. No one will notice the smoke, and if they do they will only think it's a woodman or a charcoal-burner. Here I can snare rabbits and birds. There may be other villages within reach too, so there'll be plenty to take when we want it."

Tamara looked up, smiling. She was trying to mend a tear in her clothing by means of a thin bit of wire with which she pierced holes and a piece of string which she threaded through them. She had on her feet a pair of army boots, from which her thin brown legs protruded like stalks.

" I think it would be nice to stay still at last—and live in the sun again and not always by moonlight or in the dark," she said, adding, " and not to have to be always walking."

She looked quite gay, clapping her hands and skipping a little as they set off to look for a camp site. They made a number of camps, only to destroy them and make another—rather as birds will build several nests before they think they have found exactly the right spot—until at last they discovered a dell with great trees arching over it and steep ferned banks to protect it on all sides. Close by a little stream flowed, darkly and swiftly, between moss-grown stones. There they built a hut strongly of branches, and thatched it with brushwood and the heath which grew in the clearings of the forest. Across the opening in front of the hut hung a curtain of sacking. A fireplace of stones, over which hung a cooking-pot on a triangle made out of three pieces of scrap-iron, gave the place the customary look of a gipsy camp. They had played as they made it, running and leaping like children or young animals, chasing each other with prickly bits of gorse, falling, laughing and shouting. Jean, like the boy he still was, had prankish moments when he loved to tease Tamara, but every now and then they would stop to listen when the old habit of silence and caution returned once more.

At last it was finished and they settled in, the fire was lit for the first time, and the cooking-pot made for them its first stew of rabbit, onions and potatoes, filling the glade with a smell so savoury that their mouths dribbled with hungry anticipation.

One morning Tamara was sitting before the curtained door of the hut making a basket out of willow saplings. She was singing as she worked, her face intent and happy between the long black wings of her hair.

It was hot; long shafts of sunlight filtered down upon her from between the trees. Tall ferns heavily clothed the banks now, and it would have been difficult for anyone to have found the camp unless they had come on it suddenly and from near at hand. They took care not to make a path to the place lest worn tracks should give away their whereabouts to any wandering keeper.

The girl lifted her head and listened, and in a few minutes Jean ran down the bank with a rabbit he had just taken from a snare. He flung himself down beside her to stretch out in the sun.

"Look," she said, holding up the basket, " I have two baskets now. I can make rush baskets, too."

He took it and looked at it thoughtfully. An idea struck him.

"Why shouldn't we try to sell them in the villages?" he said, turning the basket over in his hands and testing its strength. Then, as the notion grew in his mind, he added enthusiastically: "Now that's a fine idea, Tamara —I know how to make things, too. I can make pegs, clothes-pegs—I can even make flowers out of wood shavings." He looked up at her excitedly. "Oh, don't you think it's a good plan?"

For a moment she gazed back at him, her face seemed to lengthen and grow thin; doubt and then fear grew in her eyes, and she seemed to shrink.

"Oh no—no, Jean," she said, in a voice so faint

he could scarcely hear her. " It wouldn't be safe. We don't know what the people might do. We might get captured again. You know what you said—we must never be caught again ! "

But Jean was impatient. He jumped to his feet.

" What are you afraid of ? You're silly ! " He shot a disgusted glance at her. "Anyone can see the war never came here at all ! There are no soldiers. No dead men lying about—no shell-holes—no burnt houses . . . nothing ! I'm tired of this place. I want to move about—I want to be free ! "

He started to walk angrily about and kicked the rabbit into the bushes. Tamara watched him, her face piteous with anxiety as he scowled at her.

" Have you forgotten already what it was like in those awful places ? " she cried. " You weren't in one as long as I was—you didn't see what they can do to people or you might be more afraid. I *am* afraid—I'm afraid of that, and I'm afraid that they might take you away from me—and then I should be quite alone. . . ."

She began to cry. Jean swore and spat. He started to go off up the bank, but suddenly turned back to her and took her in his arms. She pushed him away with one hand and clung to him with the other ; presently his kisses turned to passion, his rough young face scrubbing against her cheeks until they grew as richly red as a hawthorn berry.

Tamara was comforted for the moment, but she knew that he was restless. She realized that now the adventure of escape was over it was no longer enough for him just to catch rabbits for her to cook, to wander in the interminable forest and prowl round the village and lonely cottages in search of food. In his journeys abroad he was now often a long time away. He had made himself a bow and some arrows, he was an extremely good shot with them, and she had been feeling more and more anxious that his bold spirit would lead to their recapture. By whom or what she did not know, nor did it greatly signify—the terror of imprisonment was the same.

With this in mind she tried to go with him on his expeditions, but he plainly wanted to go alone, telling her that women were no good at hunting anyhow, and that she made too much noise and scared his game away. So she was forced to remain near the camp, where she amused herself damming up the stream with stones and mud, or wandering off to gather willow saplings and rushes for her baskets. She was still too nervous to go far afield.

For several days after their quarrel Jean stayed at home, only going away for short visits when they needed something in the way of food. One evening he returned just before it was dark in a state of wild excitement, leaping down the bank with hair flying, clutching something beneath his coat. He ran towards her, shouting : " Guess what I've got ! You'll never guess what I've got ! "

He danced round her with extravagant caperings while Tamara stared at him open-mouthed, hand to her throat. Panting, he stopped at last in front of her.

" Go on—guess ! " he urged.

Swallowing down her apprehension, she said with a little gasp : " You've got . . . a chicken ? "

" No—better than that."

" Well—a hare then ? "

" No—no ! " His eyes gleamed with laughter and glee. " Nothing like that."

By now Tamara had caught something of his excitement, and she ran to him and tried to open his coat, under which there was something big and bulky. He hugged his coat round him and dodged her teasingly ; they laughed and wrestled.

" Be careful—you'll break it," he cried, turning his back and bending over the thing so that she could not reach it.

" Is it something alive then ? " she asked.

He shook his head.

" Well, what then ? What ? Tell me ! "

He flung open his coat and turned round.

" There now ! "

" Jean—it's a violin—a fiddle ! How did you get it ? "

He took the fiddle out from his coat and held it up to his face, twanging the strings softly.

" I stole it, of course. And I can play it too— listen. . . ."

He tuned the fiddle, and taking up the bow, began to play a little wailing gipsyish tune.

Tamara listened enchanted. She clapped her hands and began to sway her body to the time of the music.

" My father taught me," said Jean dreamily through the music. " He used to play at the fairs and for the dancing."

Music was to both of them as natural a part of their heritage as the van, the horse, the endless rumble of wheels on endless roads, so that as he played the memory of these things rose up in their minds like strange, sensuous, nostalgic ghosts. It stirred something in them both, yet neither understood ; something more than memory—an urge as ancient and natural as the migratory instinct of birds.

VI

In the vestry of the village church a meeting was taking place. The little room was crowded with people sitting on stiff, rush-seated chairs, on benches round the walls, and on the great black wooden box with its heavy wrought-iron lock that stood at one end of the vestry. Feelings were obviously running high over the subject under discussion—there was much gesticulation and excited talk. They were waiting for someone, faces kept turning towards the door in expectation and talk was hushed from time to time.

Presently a small excited boy popped his head round the door.

" He's coming now ! "

The people rose to their feet as the parish priest entered.

"Good evening, Father," they greeted him politely, and there was a pause while a chair was placed for him.

He was a tall, powerfully built man, with the reddish, weather-beaten face of a countryman, with grey eyes that usually had the suspicion of a twinkle about them. But now his face wore an expression of unwonted concern, and when they were all seated he looked round at them gravely.

"Well, my children," he said, "I have called you together tonight to discuss a matter which has been causing a great deal of talk—and some ill-feeling, I fear, has been engendered by this talk. This matter, of which I think you all know, is a serious one. We have a thief in our community."

There was a little buzz of shocked assent.

"You will all agree," he went on, "that it is time we should all meet face to face—more particularly in view of the suspicions and conjectures that have been put about amongst you. Such a thing as this has never happened before in my time with you, and I need hardly say what a great sorrow it is to me to think that one of my flock should go astray."

He paused, looking from face to face keenly. Then he continued: "Now, I want to find out which of you have definitely become aware of things stolen. . . ."

At once hubbub broke out; the whole gathering appeared to rise to its feet as he spoke, everyone wanted to speak at once. The priest held up his hand for silence.

"This matter must be properly conducted," he said sternly. "We must have order, please. Now, Madame Pinchot——" He turned to a stout, elderly woman in a corner. "You first, I think . . . ."

Madame Pinchot said excitedly that her larder window had been forced open and some butter and bacon stolen.

"I am quite sure it was not the cat," she assured them, nodding her head emphatically. "That window would have taken a strong man to get it open, I can tell you that."

She was followed by Madame Joliot, who had lost a blanket, and Mademoiselle Yvette, her daughter, who raised a titter by announcing that she had lost things from the clothes-line which she would not care to name in mixed company. The stout innkeeper had missed a bottle or two; the farrier tools from his workshop; the baker bread from his little cart, which had been left outside his house one night—and so on and so on, with the list ever being added to by the farmers or their wives, who had eggs missing and even ducks and chickens stolen. Finally the village schoolmaster announced that he had had the strangest thing of all filched from almost under his nose—his violin !

There was a gasp of amazement at this, and fresh talk bubbled up while the priest checked up his list of names. Presently he tapped for silence and peered at his flock gravely over his glasses.

"Now the interesting fact is," he said slowly, "that almost every one of you has had something taken from his or her house at one time or another during the past weeks—and, I might add, a strange variety of articles they are, too." For a second the twinkle appeared in the grey eyes, to be instantly suppressed as he bent forward to look at them seriously. "Now, please— those of you who are parents—tell me truthfully, have you any suspicion that some boy or girl has been up to mischief? Just a childish prank—a game perhaps?"

There was a hush; parents looked at one another covertly; no one spoke. A huddle of small boys grouped round the door suddenly disappeared with astonishing rapidity. Finally a buxom young woman standing at the back with her arms folded over her white apron, who was aware that a number of sly glances were being thrown in her direction, burst out with: "Oh yes—I know you are all looking at me! My Pierre may be the bad boy of the village, but all he ever took were a few apples here and there, and the curé's plums once—and besides, what would he be wanting with the schoolmaster's fiddle?"

"Yes. Yes, there is that, of course," everyone said to everyone else. "What *could* he want with the school-master's violin?"

A grey-haired man dressed in a green corduroy coat and knee-breeches got to his feet with an air of authority. It was the gamekeeper, Marche.

"Father, if I may say so," he said, blowing out and twirling his long grey moustaches, "I am of the opinion that this thief is not one of us at all—neither man, woman nor child."

"What do you put it down to, then—witchcraft?" asked an old man quizzically, and several old women crossed themselves.

"No. I think there is someone hidden in the forest who is keeping himself in food and clothes at our expense."

"Yes, that is a possibility I had also thought of," said the priest. "In fact it is most probable. Some escaped prisoner, poor soul, or some soldier in hiding."

The tension in the gathering seemed to subside, now that this idea had been propounded, though some of the women looked apprehensive.

"I suggest that I should ask the marquis to let us take the hounds out and have a run through the forest. That would be the most certain way of discovering the thief," said the keeper.

There was a rustle of excitement at this, but the priest looked doubtful.

"One would not wish to harm some poor wanderer . . ." he began.

" Don't fear, Father, the hounds would not harm a man," the keeper assured him, " but they would certainly find one if he is in the forest. They would bay and give the alarm. We must not forget, though," he added, " that he may be armed. I think some of us should take our shotguns."

"Ah—one cannot tell what desperate characters a war may not leave in its wake," said one, shaking his head wisely.

" We can't be too careful," said another.

"All the same, I should not like this idea of yours to develop into a man-hunt, Marche," said the priest, who had already sensed a rising excitement amongst the menfolk. " I will see Monsieur le Marquis myself in the morning and he will give you his instructions. In the meantime you will all lock up your houses as well as you can, and those of you who can do so must keep a good watch tonight. We may catch the thief yet— without resort to guns or dogs."

It was getting late in the evening, the shadows were leaning long across the forest glade where the now somewhat exhausted hunt was assembled. The hounds lay around, tongues lolling, or rolled in the ferns and the short green turf. Their huntsman, with his French hunting-horn over his arm, mopped his brow with a red handkerchief. The keeper propped his gun against a tree and sat down wearily. A small assembly of farmers with guns and sticks, sprawled around on their backs, looking up at the deepening sky.

"It seems we have drawn a blank, Marche," said the huntsman.

"Aye—we've covered the ground pretty well, I should say. Whoever is hiding here—if anyone is—must be deeper in the forest."

"Not quite a blank," said one of the farmers, turning over to lean on his elbow. "Jacques here has got two rabbits!"

"Ah—so he did—and he nearly added me to his bag shooting his last one," commented his neighbour.

There was a laugh at this. Old Marche stirred and stretched himself.

"We might as well go home," he said. "Getting nigh milking-time for some of you."

"Call up your hounds," said Jacques to the huntsman. "A pint of cider would go down well now, eh, Joliot?"

The huntsman sounded his horn, a long mellow note that wound its way through the forest till it died in the distance. As the company rose they suddenly heard the deep baying of a hound from somewhere far away in the forest.

"That'll be old Rosabelle," said the huntsman. "That old bitch never tires of hunting—she'd go on all night if I let her."

He blew his horn again, but the baying continued. Some of the hounds cocked their ears and started off, but were called to heel.

"Wait . . ." said the keeper. "She's speaking to something."

"What about it, boys?" asked the huntsman.

"Probably only an old boar," said one of the farmers. "Still, I'm game if the rest of you are."

"Right then." The huntsman whipped in his hounds and the pack streamed off into the trees in the direction of the baying of Rosabelle, with the company in pursuit. The hounds soon outstripped them and could presently be heard in cry.

"There is something there—they're on to something! Come on!" cried Joliot.

It did not take them long to reach the glade where Jean's and Tamara's camp was situated. There, to their astonishment, they found the pack, quiet now except for suspicious sniffings, walking round and round the little hut. Tamara and Jean stood huddled together, gazing at the hounds and looking about them in a terrified manner.

They saw the men on the bank above them almost at once, and made an instinctive movement of flight; but the keeper bawled out: "Stop! Don't move— we have you covered!"

The men plunged down the bank towards them. Tamara cowered to the ground and began to weep.

Jean stood stolidly, glowering and sullen with lowered head, making no move.

"Good God—*children*!" cried the old keeper and lowered his gun. By now the rest had come up; there was an outburst of talk as they gazed at the captives for a moment or two.

"Who are you, and what are you doing here?" Marche demanded at length.

There was a moment's silence, then: "I'm Jean and this is Tamara," Jean said in a low voice.

"Where are you from?"

Jean pointed north.

"Over there."

"Where is 'there'?" asked the keeper, frowning.

"I don't know—another country. . . ."

The men looked at one another suspiciously; there was some head-shaking and dark looks.

"They speak French," said one. "Try the girl, Marche."

"You, girl," said the old keeper. "What country do you come from?"

But Tamara was too frightened to reply. She hid her face and wept bitterly and hopelessly.

"Better see what they've got in that hut," remarked Joliot.

One of the men pulled away the sacking from the doorway and peered within.

" Here's Madame Joliot's blanket ! " he cried, dragging it forth from the bracken bed it covered.

"And look at the food ! " cried another. " There are the publican's wine bottles."

"And my wife's egg basket," exclaimed one of the farmers.

" Look—here is the schoolmaster's fiddle," said the one called Jacques, bending to pick it up. But at this Jean made a quick movement and seized the violin, which he clasped to his body with both arms. He glared at them defiantly. One of the men tried to take it from him, but Marche, seeing it might be broken in the struggle, said : " No, let him carry it—we can deal with that later."

The group set about gathering together the blanket and other things from the hut, while old Marche still stared at the two young creatures before him.

" Well, we have found the thieves, men," he said, fingering his long moustache. " Two ragged children from God knows where ! We must take them to the village at once."

" I have promised to bring whatever we find straight to the marquis," announced the huntsman.

" To the château then," said the keeper. " Quick march ! Call the hounds, Joliot, it's growing late."

Once more the horn was blown, the hounds gathered. A farmer stamped out the embers of the camp-fire,

74

and the assembly moved off down the forest ride with their two captives in their midst, Jean supporting Tamara, who still sobbed piteously.

"Don't cry, girl," said old Marche, roughly but kindly. "We will not harm you. We don't harm children."

VII

The château, like the village, was very old and grey. It had queer little turrets in the middle and at each end so that it looked as if it were a mixture of ancient fortress and château. The forest swept up to it on three sides, which, as it was built on a slight rise, gave it the effect of mysteriously hanging in space. In front of it were great lawns with dark sweeping-skirted cedars and tall black yews. Beyond the lawns an open parkland seemed to stretch into far blue distance.

There was a little gatehouse before the château, and three figures were approaching it from the long drive —two in front and one at the rear. It was Jean and Tamara with Marche, the keeper. Tamara was clinging to Jean's arm. They gazed at the old house with awe.

"Is this the prison?" whispered Tamara.

"I don't know," replied Jean, but added bravely: "Even if it is we can escape again—never fear."

They reached the gatehouse, and Marche pulled a bell which gave a cracked tingle-tangle and immediately a very old man's face appeared at a little grille in the massive gate. He peeped out at them.

"Well, Antoine—here are our thieves," announced Marche with a wink in his voice. The old man opened the gates and stared at the two, then he gave a high-pitched, wheezy laugh.

"They don't look very fierce," he said.

"Maybe not, but they had the stuff all right. We'll see what the master has to say to them, if you please," said Marche brusquely. "I'm tired and my supper is waiting for me at home this past hour."

The old man escorted them to the door of the château, at which a woman was standing waiting. She, too, was old and bent, dressed in black, with an enormously high bonnet on her head. From her waist swung a bunch of keys of many sizes and degrees of brightness.

"My God, Marche!" she cried, holding up her hands. "What have you got there? Two—so young —almost children! Where are they from? They look like wild things."

"The Lord knows where they are from—who can tell these days? They speak French, anyway—at least

77

the boy does. The girl won't speak. She cries all the time."

"Poor child—poor child. Perhaps she is hungry," said the old woman, at which Tamara lifted her eyes for the first time, to gaze at the old woman in wonder at the kind words.

"Well, we can't stop gossiping here all night," said old Marche pompously, blowing out his huge whiskers. "Take us to the master."

The old man beckoned them to follow and shuffled on before in his black felt slippers, leaving the old woman staring after them, shaking her head, with her mouth screwed up into a button. He led them into an enormous hall, on the walls of which were coats of arms, the dim reds and golds of the devices showing up darkly against their black backgrounds. Over some of them hung flags, so old they looked like nothing so much as huge spiders' webs, or like strange hanging shadows, moveless among the other shadows. In the corners stood men in armour, at which Tamara and Jean gazed with terror, believing them to be some new and terrible form of guard.

From the hall they turned down a long passage to a door at the further end. The old man knocked and listened. There was no reply, and after knocking again he opened the door and motioned to them to enter.

They found themselves in a room almost as big and shadowy as the hall. The room had long mullioned windows which let in scarcely any light, for the forest pressed up so close to them that what light there was had a mysterious greenish look like the light under the sea. A huge chandelier of crystal gleamed ghostlily from the ceiling, and the walls were peopled with shadowy faces from old, very dark portraits.

At one end was a stone fireplace in which a log fire was smouldering. Tall winged chairs stood about the hearth with their backs to the room, but when Antoine led them up to the chairs they saw that in one of them was a tiny old man asleep with a rug over his knees and his feet on a footstool. He had a little beard, and on his head was a black-velvet skull-cap. He was so tiny that he seemed little bigger than a child.

Antoine went up to him and placed a hand very lightly on the old man's shoulder.

" Sir ? " he said, and immediately the old marquis's eyes opened suddenly, like a doll's.

" What is it, Antoine—what is it ? " he asked in a voice so high and piping it was like an echo. " Not time to dine yet. . . . I know the time very well, although you think I've been asleep."

" Marche is here as you ordered, sir," said Antoine. " He has brought the thieves they have found in the forest."

"Thieves! What thieves? Poachers, I suppose you mean, old fool."

Marche came up, cap in hand, and stood before the old marquis's chair.

"No, sir, thieves. You ordered Marat to take the hounds out, if your lordship will recollect. We have caught the thieves with all the goods that were stolen. They were encamped in the forest."

The old man blinked and sat up a little in his chair.

"The devil they were," he said, rubbing his nose with a small ivory-coloured hand on which gleamed a heavy jewelled ring. "Dangerous—dangerous! They might have fired it. Yes, yes. Well, where are they, these thieves? Let me see them."

Jean and Tamara, who had been trying to edge away towards the door, were brought up to stand trembling before the old marquis's chair. He peered at them.

"I can't see them well. Poke the fire, Antoine— bring candles."

The fire was made to blaze and a three-branched silver candelabra was placed on the table beside his chair. The old man took it up and bent towards Tamara and Jean.

"Come closer," he commanded, and they approached timidly, to be scrutinized by a pair of remarkably bright black eyes set in a face as wrinkled as an old seed. The two young people stared back at him with all the innocent curiosity of very young children or animals—and with eyes equally black, bright and inscrutable.

After a moment the old man replaced the candelabra; then he chuckled—the oddest little high-pitched chuckle, which ceased as suddenly as it had begun. His face changed and became stern.

"Where do you come from and what were you doing in my forest, young man?" he asked Jean. "Who are you?"

"I am Jean and this is Tamara," replied the boy for the second time that day. But there was no surliness in his reply this time.

"Ho—you speak French, then? Well, where are you come from?"

Jean shook his head.

"I don't know," he answered truthfully.

The old man frowned.

"You don't know? Have a care, boy. I will not allow insolence."

"I have already asked them that question, sir," interposed Marche. "The boy will not say."

"Silence, Marche," said the old marquis imperiously, and then to Jean: "How did you come to be in the forest? Answer me."

"We came a long way—many nights and many days. We travelled by night and hid by day."

"From what direction did you come?"

" From the north."

The old man nodded.

" Ah, so you know that much, then. From the north, eh ? And was this girl with you all the time ? "

" Yes."

" Say sir to his lordship, you young ruffian," growled Marche.

" Sir," said Jean.

"And why were you hiding by day ? "

" We were afraid they would capture us again and take us back to prison."

There was a moment's pause. Marche and Antoine glanced at one another.

" Oh, so you were in prison, were you ? " said the marquis thoughtfully, but not angrily. " You must be very bad young people to be in prison at your age. And why were you in prison ? Thieving, I suppose ? "

Jean made no reply to this, hung his head and looked sullen, but Tamara now came suddenly forward, clasping her hands beseechingly.

" Oh, please—oh, please don't send us back, your majesty," she cried, convinced that the old man must be at the very least a king. " We are not thieves. The Germans put us in prison—we don't know why ! They killed our fathers and mothers, our brothers and sisters. I was in prison a long time. They beat us and gave us no food—they killed a lot of us. Then

Jean came with a lot more prisoners, and later on a lot of different soldiers—not German—and Jean and I ran away. We hadn't done anything wrong. Oh, please believe us. Please, please don't send us back ! "

She began to cry and tremble violently. Jean put his arm round her shaking shoulders and looked defiantly at the old marquis and the two servants.

All three stared at the two young, ragged, unkempt creatures before them ; then the old man took out an enormous handkerchief and wiped his eyes.

"Oh, my poor children—poor little ones." His voice quavered. "I understand now. I understand it all. Antoine, what are you gaping at ? Fetch some wine at once." He turned to Tamara and reached out to hand her his handkerchief. "Don't cry, child. Don't you understand—the Germans are *our* enemies also. You will never be sent back. We must try and find out if you have anyone alive belonging to you—any relatives—and what part of our dear France you are from." He broke off, muttering to himself : "My God, what a history—these poor children. *What* a foe to ill-treat children." Then aloud he added : "But we must deal with matters of the present. You have been stealing from my people. That was wrong. What have you there under your coat, boy ? "

"It is the schoolmaster's violin, sir," said old Marche, stepping forward. "He will not give it up. We were afraid to take it from him by force lest it should be broken."

"That is a strange thing for a boy to take," said the marquis. "Hand it over at once, boy—d'you understand?"

Slowly and reluctantly Jean drew the fiddle out from under his coat. The old man reached out to take it when an idea struck him.

"No—wait. Can ye play it, boy?"

Instantly a smile lit up Jean's gipsy face, his white teeth flashed a brilliant half-moon.

"Oh yes! Oh yes, I play! . . . Shall I play now? Listen!"

Flinging back his hair and striking a dramatic attitude, Jean lifted the violin, made a great sweep with his bow and played a wild gipsy tune—old and haunting, gay and sad. The notes seemed to curl about the room, disturbing the shadows, shivering amongst the trembling crystal drops of the chandelier; the dark faces of the portraits seemed to lean out of their heavy gilt frames as if astonished at this strange, unwonted sound.

The old man was delighted. He nodded to the music and clapped his hands.

"Bravo! Bravo! Antoine, Marche, these young creatures shall stay with me until something about their history can be traced. No, no!" He waved an imperious hand at Antoine, who he perceived was about to make gestures of demur. "Antoine, lay two extra places at table and tell Marthe to have rooms prepared. Marche, you may go. . . ."

" But, your lordship—the schoolmaster's violin . . . ? "

" Drat the schoolmaster ! He must do without it for the time. This boy shall play for me, and the girl shall sing after we have dined. They shall be my troubadours. You'll like that, eh ? " He looked at Tamara. " You'll sing for an old man, eh ? " He chuckled, and then the chuckle suddenly became a querulous, cross old voice. " I'm tired now. Go—all of you. Go, I say ! Send Marthe to me. I want my shawl. I'm cold—I'm tired. . . ."

Tamara and Jean moved towards the door, with the two servants following. The two men paused at the door and looked back indecisively. Their heads wagged and their faces were full of concern as Marche said under his breath : " The master is childish . . . it will never do ! "

" These children are savages."

" He can't realize—— "

" Perhaps Marthe will be able to get some sense into him," whispered Antoine.

Marthe, the old woman, was waiting for them, just outside the door.

" You heard, of course ? " asked Antoine.

"Yes, I heard." The old woman looked with compassion at Jean and Tamara, who now stood close together against the wall, so young, so forlorn, so frightened even yet—but she, too, shook her head. "No—it will certainly *not* do. Best leave it for now. No use crossing the old man tonight."

Tomorrow, yes, but not when he was tired. To get him into one of his rages at night would be disastrous, she thought. She would find these ragged young ones some clean garments and somewhere to sleep—would try to make them wash. And they must pray God that events would shape themselves in a more seemly manner in course of time. He would soon forget—he was like a child, so old—so old. . . .

VIII

Many and long were the confabulations between Marthe
and Antoine in the days that followed. They talked at
their meals in the vast vaulted kitchen that lay under
the château; they came together to confer at odd
moments during the days, when a fresh cause for alarm
took them; they talked far into the nights long after
old Antoine had blown the candle out, though they
would often light it again with the subconscious hope
in their minds that its little glow would light some
fresh avenue of hope as yet unexplored by them. But
it never did, and at last Antoine would pull his night-
cap down over his ears, turn his back on his wife and
try to go to sleep.

Nothing they could say or do seemed to be any good. Matters had become completely out of hand, for the old marquis, far from being reasonable, was now quite determined not to part with his protégés, and flew into rages when approached—even going so far as to throw his stick at Antoine on more than one occasion, and being very shaky and childish himself for hours afterwards.

When Marthe tried to inform him of what danger he was in by harbouring two such suspicious raga-muffins, her admonishings and warnings had been met by an uncontrollable burst of laughter.

" They even sleep together—and what's more, not in the bed, but on the floor ! " she told him with shocked disapproval. "And when I insisted that they should sleep in different rooms they would not do so. They said they were married. Married ! " she snorted. " The good God alone knows what they are or where they have come from."

But the old man merely seemed to think this shocking immorality was a new delicious joke, so that Marthe, in the end, hurried from the room in a flood of angry weeping to confide to Antoine that the old man was off his head.

Jean and Tamara, after the first night of fear and doubt, when they had discussed the idea of escaping from the château, had examined with awe the great canopied beds that Marthe had provided for them in separate rooms. They felt the soft sheets and coverings, the thick mattresses; had fingered the long crimson curtains with wonder. Tamara drew the curtains round the beds with delight.

" Why, it makes another little room ! "

But they dragged some of the bedding off the bed and away into one corner to make a bed on the floor, where Marthe discovered them the next morning, to her shocked dismay.

In a few days they had lost all fear of the old marquis. They became wildly happy. They were completely unconcerned now about the future, and the past was forgotten. They ran about the ancient château, or in the deserted stables and grounds. At night they sang and Jean played his fiddle for the old marquis, and they laughed together, all three of them, like children. They drank the wine that Antoine was forced to pour out for them at mealtimes—rare red wine in ancient, exquisite goblets—and ate whatever was put before them—with their fingers.

" They are *savages*," said Antoine to Marthe.

Long days were spent by them wandering from room to room in the château, although the old woman did her best to keep all the rooms locked. She was no match for Jean, who stole the keys from her as easily as he might have taken an egg from beneath a sitting hen. Strange, enchanted rooms they entered, shuttered and sheeted and quiet with the silence of empty years. Some were magnificent with tapestries and beautiful ornaments and full of heavy, antique furniture. Some were quaint, delicately furnished in faint colours that had long since faded—frail, feminine rooms upholstered in satins of palest rose, dim blues and greys. About these there seemed to hang the ghosts of perfumes.

There was one room lined with books from floor to ceiling. Other rooms were dark and strange, with windows that were hung over by long curtains of ivy outside, giving a green, sea-like gloom within and where dusty mirrors gleamed spectrally.

The attics, which seemed to be countless, and which had at one time housed the staff, were, however, filled with light. They were above the level of the trees and seemed packed with the dusty, broken furniture of centuries—old shapeless beds, queer, unidentifiable bundles, discarded pictures—the flotsam of the years lying now forgotten in the pools of mote-filled sunlight of the endless afternoons, washed by the smouldering moonlight in the ageless nights.

Long corridors, narrow passages, twisting unexpected stairs led hither and thither, so that they began to believe that there was no end to these mysterious, spellbound chambers.

In many of the bedrooms there were huge wardrobes and chests filled with clothes, all of bygone fashions; men's and women's clothes of rich velvets and brocades, cloaks of stiff wool cloth, heavily embroidered with gold threads or frogged across the fronts with scarlet. Hunting clothes, ball gowns, frail summer dresses that spoke of hot afternoons in drowsy gardens —all smelled of some strange spicy perfume when Jean and Tamara pulled them from their chests and shook them out.

They spent an afternoon dressing themselves in these garments and admiring themselves in the long mirrors. In the evening they displayed themselves in their finery to the marquis, who was as pleased at their fantastic appearance as a child at a pantomime.

He called them his " jesters "—and indeed that was the role they filled in the lonely old man's life. At times he would not remember who they were and would call them by strange names—the names of friends and relatives of his past. He would often fall asleep suddenly in the middle of a sentence, to believe on waking that they were part of some dream that had been drifting through his muddled old head. Now and then he would become testy and irritable and send them off with imperious gestures of dismissal.

When this happened Antoine and Marthe would become more hopeful; but the next evening he would send for his " jesters " again, with an insistence equally imperious. Jean and Tamara obeyed his dismissals and summonses with calm equanimity. They still believed him to be a king, though they had long lost all fear of him. They treated him now with a kind of affectionate indulgence, and with the understanding that the innocent young sometimes have for the very old. For innocent they were in essence, though now grown out of childhood physically. Both had witnessed scenes of hideous brutality, rape, horrors of all kinds, and seen death at its most obscene. They had known fear so paralysing that the mind seems to dissolve and run out with the cold sweat of one's terror. Both had known pain, hunger, cold, as well as the infinite anguish of imprisonment and its grey dolours of monotony. Yet because of that core of innocence and wildness that was in them they were in some way impervious to these things. They had come through untouched in spirit, being able to accept the fact of evil and that such things could happen to you if you were unlucky enough to be caught by war. They were like birds, able to accept the cage and see the bird in the next cage torn to pieces by the cat, and yet must sing at the first wild stirrings of spring.

In their old patron of ancient and noble lineage there lay, strangely enough, a spirit akin to this—a long-dormant seed that responded and reached out tenuous, delicate tendrils to these young gipsies—something long hidden and obscured by the years but which had flourished in his youth.

The house, with its rooms full of treasure, was not the only source of joy to Tamara and Jean. They wandered endlessly in the grounds, in the great overgrown gardens, the conservatories with their vines hanging untended from their rotting staples. They sat in the little ruined summerhouses and delicate white-marble follies that were columned and fluted and decorated with cherubs. They ran along the terraces to gaze in wonder at the stone figures of the fountain that looked as if they were struggling through a breaking wave of roses and briars.

All this sunlit, luxuriant decay was to them both a playground. Its haunted noonday somnolence, its languorous mists at evening held for them not a hint of melancholy. All was gay—not a whisper of age or death—in the dim old rooms of the château, where nothing had moved for years but the drifting dust-motes in the thick yellow sun-rays. All was gay in the silent gardens, undisturbed by any movement save a bird's wings or a wind-borne thistle seed.

They did, however, discover one living and friendly being—a fat old mare, left solitary in stables built to house thirty or forty horses. She was as pleased to see them as they were to find her, and greeted them with stampings and whinnies when they visited her there, or in the paddock, with food—titbits of bread or sugar. Jean would run his hands over her and feel her legs with the air of a man knowledgeable about horses—which indeed he was.

Perhaps best of all they liked the coach-houses, which were filled with every kind of equipage from delicately sprung, spindly-wheeled gigs and phaetons to magnificent carriages and great coaches with coats of arms emblazoned upon them. They were all thick with dust and cobwebs, which would rise in clouds in the long beams of sunlight that streamed through the slatted windows when they entered.

There was one vehicle in particular that they loved most dearly. This was a kind of covered wagon, designed, no doubt, to carry game home from shooting expeditions, or deer and boar from the forest hunting, but it suggested in every aspect a gipsy caravan. Jean liked to climb into the driver's seat of this wagon or sit on the shaft gipsy fashion while Tamara sat inside. They would look at one another and laugh—or sigh—and say nothing. There was no need for words. Memories, dreams, filled their thoughts, for the wagon, like the fiddle, Tamara's baskets, the horse, was a part of their natural heritage—something of which a world at war had so cruelly and incomprehensibly robbed them.

IX

In strange, dream-like sequence the days went by for Tamara and Jean in this world of the past, which the tides of war had swept around and left islanded and almost untouched.

One evening the old marquis, in a mood of melancholy, did not want his troubadours to play or sing for him. He was in a talkative mood, rambling back into his past in ancient, disconnected reminiscences, pausing now and then to take a sip of brandy and nod off into a drowse, only to wake and begin again when a log falling in the fire roused him.

"I am a very old man," he told them. "A very old man indeed. My dear wife died many many years ago. I do not think I shall live very much longer, my children.

Nor do I wish to, for Antoine and Marthe are getting old too and cannot serve me much longer. My son, my only son, died fighting for France in the war. Was it this war? No, no—it couldn't have been. . . ." His voice died into incoherent mutterings as he tried to bring his mind to focus on the recollection of his son's death. " No—it must have been the last war in 1914— yes, I remember now. . . . There is no one left—I am a very lonely old man. I forget things; all the days are alike to me now. Yes, it is time I went . . . time I went."

The two young people gazed at him sorrowfully, while the old man rambled.

" Do not be sad," Tamara said to him gently. " Would you like me to dance for you—or shall I sing softly? Or shall we dress up for you? How you did laugh at Jean in his funny hat and great boots. . . ."

The marquis shook his head.

" No, girl—I like sometimes to talk of the past and of my son. That is his portrait there——" He turned to point at one of the pictures on the wall beside them, the painting of a dark, thin young man with a little black moustache and bright, vivacious dark eyes. He was dressed in a uniform with red and gold trimmings and had a look that was both gallant and gay and a little whimsical. " That is his portrait, and his sword hangs by it," the old man went on, and sighed. "Ah, my splendid son. . . . We have had so many wars. This old house has been besieged more than once in its history. He died for France, and his tomb is in the church, though I have not been there to see it for many years. My dear wife—my Clothilde—is with him there, and soon I shall lie there likewise."

The girl rose suddenly and moved over to the old man and knelt by his chair. Jean folded his arms and tried to look brave and stern, as befitted a man. The marquis began to nod again, then after a while he continued; his speech had become slower now, for his emotion had tired him. The girl tried to make him stop talking and motioned to Jean that it was time they went away and left him to rest, but as they began to tiptoe away he roused once more and beckoned them to return.

He sat up a little in his chair, leaning forward and looking from one to the other.

"When I am gone," he said at last with a sudden unexpected return of vigour, "I want you to stay on here. You shall have the château, my children. No one else cares for it—there is no one to care for it. You shall have it all. I will make it possible—I will see my attorney. You shall have it all—everything—the estate, the furniture, the books, the pictures, the horses, the stables—all of it. You shall hunt, Jean—and shoot with my guns in the forest. You'll like that, eh?

And the girl, Tamara, shall have all the clothes and the jewels she loves so much to dress in—eh? All girls love clothes, don't they, eh, my pretty? Smile now, smile. No more tears for your old king. You'll like that, won't you? You'll like all those things . . . ?"

"The carriage!" said Jean suddenly. "Can we have the carriage?"

"Yes, yes, yes—all the carriages and the horses," said the old marquis, quite forgetting that his stables now contained but one old stout black Flemish mare that Antoine occasionally harnessed to fetch potatoes or flour from the village.

Tamara kissed the old man's hand very softly. He was already dozing, and this time they were able to steal from the room without waking him. But the tiny noise of the closing door aroused him and he rang for Antoine.

"I want you to write a letter for me," he commanded when the old servant had entered the room.

Antoine hesitated and looked surprised, for although he always wrote the marquis's infrequent letters for him this was not the usual time for such business to take place.

"It is getting late, sir," he said. "It is time for you to retire. I'm afraid it will tire you to write a letter now, and Marthe will scold me——"

"Mind your own business," said his old master

testily, " and do as I bid you. I want it done now—
tonight—at once."

With some ceremony and a good deal of muttered
grumbling on the part of one old man, the candle for
sealing, the wax, the pens and paper were assembled.
After much testing of the pen and adjusting of the
candle, Antoine was at last ready for dictation and the
letter was begun. As it progressed Antoine became
more and more filled with consternation. He fidgeted
and twisted in his chair ; he ran his fingers through his
stubbly grey hair until it was literally standing on end ;
he paused and stared wildly at his master. He could
scarcely write, so shaky had his hand become. The
marquis glanced up at him, thumping on the floor with
his stick. He grew angry.

" What in the name of ten thousand devils is the
matter with you, Antoine ? " he cried, and banged his
stick across the table, making the candle jump and the
grease spill on the paper.

" Oh, sir ! Oh, master . . ." stuttered the servant.
" Do you . . . ? Are you sure . . . ?"

" How dare you presume to question me ? " shouted
the old marquis, trembling himself now. " Proceed at
once. God's teeth, what are things coming to ? Go
on—go on ! Immediately ! "

The letter was continued, with Antoine's writing
becoming scarcely legible with his agitation.

At last it was finished and duly sealed.

"Bring wine," the marquis commanded, and Antoine actually spilled some in pouring it from the decanter and setting the goblet by his master.

"Clumsy old oaf!" growled the old man to him. "You are growing older and sillier every day." He fell back in his chair and passed his hands wearily over his face. "Ah dear—ah dear me! Send Marthe to me. My feet are cold. I want the footwarmer. Send Marthe. I want to go to bed."

Antoine almost scuttled from the room.

He went at a shambling trot down the passage, down the wide stone stairs to the cavernous kitchens below, calling as he pushed open the kitchen door: "Marthe! Marthe! Come quickly...."

Marthe appeared with an anxious face and clutching her apron.

"The master... is he...?"

"No, no—not what you think," cried Antoine. "Worse—far worse!"

"What, then, for God's sake... not the Germans again?"

"No, you old fool! It is something terrible...."

The old woman tottered forward, her eyes wide with fear.

"Not—not a fire?"

"No—no... a letter!" Antoine was walking up

and down, gesticulating as he went. His wife dropped her hands from her cheeks and looked at him with scorn.

"A letter? Is that all? Well, it is you who is the fool—all this fuss over a letter. Calm yourself. Sit down. Let me see this letter."

Antoine flung himself into a chair and threw the letter on the table.

"Everything!" he cried. "He is giving them *everything*! He is mad—he is in his dotage! Everything is lost. . . . And what is to become of us, I should like to know?"

Marthe fumbled in her dress for her spectacles and looked at the address on the envelope.

"But this is to his lawyer," she said. "This is quite ordinary. You write one for him every month—and have done these many years."

Antoine heaved round in his chair and looked at her, with frustrated disgust at her stupidity overcoming for the moment his despair.

"Yes—but you don't know what is in this one," he told her with heavy emphasis. "He is making a new will. He is leaving them everything—the château, the estate, the silver and gold plate . . . the whole place. Everything. My God, what a thing to happen—what a thing!"

"Leaving everything to whom? What do you mean —to whom?"

"To them—those savages—those children—those gipsies!"

"My God!"

It was now Marthe's turn to sit down with a bump on the chair opposite her husband. There was a pause. They gazed at one another, old faces haggard with dismay.

"What a disaster! Oh, that we should have lived to see such a thing!" groaned Antoine at last. "What can we do? Can't you think of anything, old woman? What is to become of us if this is to come about? He cannot last much longer—that is the danger. There may be little time to act."

But Marthe, who had always been the one to take control in times of crisis and whose sly woman's wit her husband had always secretly respected, seemed as overwhelmed as he. She sat motionless in her chair, her legs stuck out before her and her eyes wandering aimlessly over the stone-flagged floor of the kitchen. She put a hand over her eyes, pushing her bonnet to the back of her head.

"Wait while I think. The old master is certainly in his dotage or he would never have done such a thing. He cannot know what he is doing. Those rascals—those ruffians! They must have got hold of him!"

She cast her apron over her head and began to rock to and fro. Antoine watched her anxiously, and presently her face reappeared from behind the apron. She was calmer now; an idea had come to her and she was prepared to take command of the situation.

"You must go straight and see Father Benoit," she told her husband, "now—at once. We must tell him all that has taken place tonight. He will arrange to see the attorney. But not a word to those ruffians, you understand? Not a word—not one syllable—nor to the old master, you understand? Not one word. Act as if nothing had happened."

At that moment one of the bells of the long row that hung near the ceiling along the wall jangled violently, and the old couple jumped to their feet as if shot.

"My God!" cried Antoine. "I forgot. He wanted his footwarmer—hurry! Hurry!"

"You go straight to see the Father now before we have to post this letter. He will know what to do."

She began to bustle about filling an ancient copper warming-pan with hot water from an enormous black kettle which stood on the hob of the stove. Antoine crammed on his beret and went out without another word. The bell jangled again.

"My God, my God! What a disaster—what a thing! I must get him to his bed before anything else happens," she muttered, and hurried from the room.

The pale pearly light of early dawn filtered through the long stone-mullioned windows of Jean's and Tamara's bedroom, touching the heavy dark furniture with a milky lustre. It stole over the great bed with its curtains of faded crimson damask, the tall wardrobe that reached to the grey moulded ceiling, the big bow-legged chairs that stood before the empty cavernous hearth; it gleamed dustily in the dressing-table mirror that, tilted a little upwards, reflected from outside the window the top of a cedar tree and a stretch of calm, pale sky.

This dim milky light also lit up a scene of extra-ordinary activity—Jean and Tamara were packing.

On the floor lay a bundle of rolled-up bedding and scattered around it a strange assortment of articles—a kettle, some pots and pans, cups and plates of different colours and designs, a blue enamel can with a lid, and Tamara's baskets strung together with string by their handles. Tamara kept talking to Jean eagerly in whispers and flitting in and out of the door, to return at intervals with fresh treasures in her hands to be included in the bundle Jean was tying up in one corner of the room. He paused to examine them as she held them out to him, but mostly he waved them away—queer things girls always wanted to hold on to, he thought scornfully.

She vanished, to reappear as Jean was tying up the bedding with rope. She was wearing a long black outlandish-looking mantle that reached to her feet; in her hand was a wide-brimmed hat with a feather plume. She exhibited the hat shyly, smiling her eager, half-wistful smile.

"Jean," she said, "do you think I could take this cloak—and this hat?" She looked at it admiringly. "It is such a beautiful hat."

Jean glanced at it casually.

"Yes, I should think so," he answered. "He did say he was going to give us everything. I'm sure he wouldn't mind if you took the hat."

Tamara tried the hat on in front of the looking-glass. Her little face peeped back at her darkly from the shadowy glass. She stood there for so long that Jean stopped his roping to look up at her.

"What's wrong now?" he asked impatiently.

She turned to face him, a quaint figure with serious eyes suddenly questioning.

"Jean—I am wondering . . ." she said at last, slowly, as a thought began to take hold of her. "Do you really think we should leave him? I'm afraid he will be lonely now if we go. He likes us to be here. He will be sad when we go."

But Jean shook his head.

"No," he answered, and she could see he was quite determined. "No. It is time for us to go. I want to go. I want to move on. I want to see the world. We can't always stay here—I don't want to. I want to get on the road."

"But d'you think it's safe now—really safe? We shan't be put in prison again?" Her lip trembled as she took off the huge hat and fingered the feather.

"Of course not!" He was scornful again. "The war is over. There are no guns, no soldiers—not even an aeroplane hardly."

She was still not entirely convinced.

"But how shall we live?"

"Oh—you are silly! How did we live all that time we were travelling—and in the forest? Besides, we can sell things now—your baskets and things. And there will sure to be fairs. I can play at them like my father used to—we shall be rich—we shall have children. Then we will come back and see him. He'll remember us—he'll like to see us then, Tamara."

Tamara nodded thoughtfully. She rather liked the picture that his words had conjured up in her mind, but she added gravely: "All the same, I don't think we ought to leave him like this—without even thanking him, Jean. He is so good and kind to us."

Jean tied the last knot on his bundle and stood up to straighten his back and stand for a moment, his black eyebrows drawn together in thought.

"Could we write a letter?" he suggested suddenly. "Can you write, Tamara?"

She clapped her hands.

" Oh yes ! I think so. There's some paper and pens in that tiny room in the tower. Wait—I'll get them. . . ."

She hurried from the room, to return with a piece of paper and a heavy silver inkpot and pen.

After much discussion and cogitation the letter was finished at last. Jean looked at it admiringly.

" Where shall we put it ? " asked the girl.

" Here, on the table. Marthe will find it—she'll give it to him." Jean put it on the table under a tall branched candlestick in which the candles were still burning, a pallid flame in the growing light. He blew out the flames and a tiny spiral of smoke drifted from them.

" Come on now—it's time," said Jean.

In the dim mushroom light of the dewy meadow the old Flemish mare snorted at Jean, surprised at being approached at such an unaccustomed hour. He took her by the forelock and led her into the cobbled yard opposite the coach-houses, where Tamara was waiting surrounded by bundles. She held the horse while Jean harnessed her, then together they dragged the covered game-wagon from the coach-house. In a few moments the mare was in the shafts, the bundles were put inside the wagon and the string of Tamara's baskets and the pots and pans were tied on behind and they were ready to depart.

Tamara climbed in and Jean mounted the driver's seat and gathered up the reins, when Tamara suddenly clutched his arm.

" Oh, wait, Jean—wait a moment ! " she begged, her voice once more tremulous with anxiety. " You are *sure* we are doing right ? We aren't stealing, are we ? Not this time . . . ? "

" No ; we can't be," Jean assured her stoutly. " He did say we could have *all* the carriages and horses. We only wanted one. He said we could have everything. Get on, Violette ! " He slapped the reins on the fat back of the mare and the wagon rumbled away out of the courtyard.

Marthe's movements about the kitchen that morning were slow ; she felt unusually feeble and old and wanted nothing so much as a nice hot cup of coffee, but had not the heart to make one for herself. She raked out the ashes of the kitchen fire in an absentminded and desultory fashion, leaving them scattered in an untidy heap in the hearth. The sense of disaster and change was heavy upon her, and she paused frequently to sit back on her heels and stare into space, the dust rising in clouds about her. Her mind was full of conjectures, and not one of them was hopeful. Once or twice her hands strayed to her bunch of keys—her badge of office and responsibility—and she shook her head while slow, old-woman's tears welled from her eyes and fell into the ashes.

Antoine came into the kitchen carrying a tray on which were the remains of the marquis's breakfast. She looked up at him dully.

"How is the master this morning?"

"No different from any other morning," replied the old man. He sat down wearily by the stove. His attitude of dejection roused his wife, and she looked at him sharply.

"Now, Antoine—no sitting about this morning. We have work to do, with the Father coming here directly." She got up and, seizing a broom, began to sweep violently round his feet as if suddenly bewitched into action. "Get on—do!" She stopped sweeping for a moment to listen, her face becoming suffused with anger. "Those ruffians are very quiet this morning. I have prepared their meal. Go upstairs and rouse them. I feel as if I could not bring myself to look at them, much less feed them."

Antoine pulled himself out of the chair and went off; Marthe carried the breakfast tray out into the pantry. Before she had started to wash up she heard the shuffling footsteps of her husband returning—hurrying this time. He burst into the kitchen.

"Marthe," he called, "they are not there!"

His wife reappeared with the dishcloth in her hands, leaving a little trail of water on the flags behind her.

" Not there ? What do you mean, old man ? "

" They are not in the room—and what's more, there are no bedclothes on the bed. And I found this paper on the table. Read it, woman—I can't find my spectacles —read it for God's sake. Something has happened ! "

The old woman took the paper to the window. She peered at it, put it down and stared at her husband, then took it up again. Antoine, who had now found his glasses, snatched it from her. He read aloud : " Thank you for the carriage and the horse."

The paper fell from his trembling hand. They gazed at one another, their faces blank. The dripping dishcloth made a widening pool upon the floor.

" Well ! " said Marthe at last. She was incapable of any further syllable.

" They've gone," Antoine said in hushed tones as realization broke through his bewilderment. " They've gone—do you understand, old woman ? They've made off ! D'you hear ? "

" May the good God be thanked," said old Marthe devoutly, and crossed herself. " What a deliverance ! What a mercy ! Oh, what an escape from disaster ! "

Their ancient faces shone with relief and happiness until the old woman's, at a sudden thought, clouded over.

" But how are we to break it to his lordship ? "

Antoine shook his head dumbly and looked stupid.

"You will have to tell him they've gone."

"No. Better for you to—after his morning nap," said his wife firmly, rejecting the plea in his voice. "The poor old master. They did at least bring a little gaiety into his life—those ragamuffins."

A look of compassion came into her face for a moment, to be quickly dispelled by the expression of angry resentment habitual to her whenever she thought of Jean and Tamara.

Antoine had picked up the paper again and was reading it as she went on speaking.

"Perhaps it would be best if the Father broke the news to him. What do you think, Antoine?"

But Antoine paid no heed to her words. He flung the paper on the floor and clutched his head; he stamped; he gesticulated wildly so that Marthe believed for a moment that he had taken leave of his senses.

"My God—Marthe! This letter! It says the carriage and the *horse*! I never thought till now—do you know what that means? They have taken Violette . . . my Violette!"

He sank down into his chair, his face distraught. His wife continued to stare at him, her mouth slowly falling open. Then she began to laugh.

"Be quiet, you silly stupid old man! As if one old horse mattered! Indeed you should be ashamed of yourself—going on so. Just think what they might have taken? Think what we have been saved from? Well—of all the silly old babies. . . ."

But the old fellow refused to be comforted. He moaned and groaned and rubbed his hands over his face.

" My Violette . . . my Violette . . . ."

Along a hot white road of France between dusty hedges rumbled the wagon. Violette plodded contentedly along, the wagon swaying and the pots and pans swinging at the back. Jean walked by the horse. He whistled as he went. He had a flower in the side of his cap. Inside Tamara sat, looking dreamily forward at the road ahead.

The horizon stretched before them, wide and clear under an immense arch of sky. They were clear of the forest.